ellington

was

not

a street

WRITTEN BY NTOZAKE SHANGE

ILLUSTRATIONS BY KADIR NELSON

SIMON & SCHUSTER BOOKS FOR YOUNG READERS
NEW YORK   LONDON   TORONTO   SYDNEY   SINGAPORE

SIMON & SCHUSTER BOOKS FOR YOUNG READERS
An imprint of Simon & Schuster Children's Publishing Division
1230 Avenue of the Americas, New York, New York 10020
Text copyright © 1983 by Ntozake Shange
Illustrations copyright © 2004 by Kadir Nelson
All rights reserved, including the right of
reproduction in whole or in part in any form.
SIMON & SCHUSTER BOOKS FOR YOUNG READERS
is a trademark of Simon & Schuster, Inc.
Book design by Paula Winicur and Dan Potash
The text of this book is set in Filosofia.
The illustrations are rendered in oils.
Manufactured in China
10 9 8 7 6 5 4 3
Library of Congress Cataloging-in-Publication Data
Shange, Ntozake.
Ellington was not a street / by Ntozake Shange ; illustrated by Kadir Nelson.
p. cm.
ISBN 0-689-82884-5
1. Afro-American civil rights workers—Juvenile poetry. 2. Afro-American artists—
Juvenile poetry. 3. Afro-American girls—Juvenile poetry. 4. Children's poetry,
American. [1. Afro-Americans—Poetry. 2. American poetry.] I. Nelson, Kadir, ill.
II. Title.
PS3569.H3324 E45 2002
811'.54—dc21   00-045060

The poem "Mood Indigo" is reprinted from *A Daughter's Geography*,
published by St. Martin's Press, Inc., New York, NY.

To my beloved father and well-loved mother, Paul and Eloise Williams;
To my sisters, Ifa and Bisa;
To my brother, Paul, and his wife, Aimee—

For what our lives were
And what we wish our children's lives to be
—N. S.

For my dad, Lenwood Melvin Nelson
—K. N.

it hasnt always been this way
ellington was not a street

robeson no mere memory

hummed some tune over me
sleeping in the company of men
who changed the world

it wasnt always like this

why ray barretto used to be a side-man
& dizzy's hair was not always grey

i remember   i was there
i listened in the company of men

politics as necessary as collards
music even in our dreams

our house was filled with all kinda folks
our windows were not cement or steel

our doors opened like our daddy's arms
held us safe & loved

children growing in the company of men
old southern men & young slick ones

sonny til was not a boy
the clovers no rag-tag orphans
our crooners/ we belonged to a whole world

nkrumah was no foreigner
virgil akins was not the only fighter

it hasnt always been this way
ellington was not a street

More about a few of the men
"who changed the world"

PAUL ROBESON (b. April 9, 1898; d. January 23, 1976) Actor. Singer. Athlete. Activist. In 1915 Robeson won a four-year scholarship to Rutgers University, becoming the third African American to attend. While at Rutgers, Robeson played on the football team, won contests for his public-speaking skills, and graduated valedictorian, delivering the class speech. Known as a Renaissance man, Robeson also had artistic talent. He played the leading roles in such plays as *All God's Chillun Got Wings* and *The Emperor Jones* by Eugene O'Neill. He was also in one of the longest-running productions of *Othello* in Broadway history. Musically, he dominated songs such as "Ol' Man River" with his powerful voice, becoming nationally as well as internationally known. Throughout his career he constantly showed his determination to help others by speaking against racism and fascism.

WILLIAM EDWARD BURGHARDT (W. E. B.) DuBOIS (b. February 23, 1868; d. August 27, 1963) Historian. Sociologist. Writer. Along with graduating from high school at the age of sixteen, DuBois also became the first African American to receive a doctorate from Harvard University. In his career he researched and wrote about the historical and social conditions of the African Americans in society, authoring such works as *The Suppression of the African Slave-Trade to the United States of*  *America, 1638–1870* (1896), *The Philadelphia Negro* (1899), *The Souls of Black Folk* (1903), and *Black Reconstruction* (1935). His research helped bring social consciousness and was valuable in the development of the National Association for the Advancement of Colored People (better known as the NAACP). In 1910 DuBois became one of the NAACP's founding officers, maintaining membership until 1934. In 1961 he became editor-in-chief of *Encyclopedia Africana*, which he worked on during his stay in Africa. He died in Ghana in 1963.

RAY BARRETTO (b. April 29, 1929) Percussionist. Among the very first musicians to incorporate conga drums into jazz. From early in his career Ray Barretto showed his talent for playing jazz and salsa. In 1957 he played drums for Tito Puente before going on to lead his own band and record his own records. Frequently named the Best Conga Player of the Year by *Latin NY* magazine, Barretto received greater recognition by winning a Grammy nomination in 1976 for his album *Barretto*. In 1990 he was nominated again and this time won the Grammy Award for his album with salsa legend Celia Cruz. He was inducted into the International Latin Music Hall of Fame in 1999 and continues to record music today.

EARLINGTON CARL "SONNY TIL" TILGHMAN (b. August 18, 1928; d. December 9, 1981) Singer. Lead vocalist of the rhythm and blues group the Orioles from the 1940s to the 1950s. The group helped pave the way for other rhythm and blues and doo-wop groups. Although The Orioles separated in 1954, Sonny Til continued recording with some of its members until 1981.

JOHN BIRKS "DIZZY" GILLESPIE (b. October 21, 1917; d. January 6, 1993) Jazz Trumpeter. Composer. Among the early players of bebop. He was instrumental in introducing modern jazz to the use of conga drums to develop the Afro-Cuban beat, and was one of the early players of Latin jazz. In 1956 he was recommended to President Dwight D. Eisenhower to lead a good-will orchestra tour through various countries, including South Africa. Throughout his career he played with jazz greats such as Charlie Parker, Ella Fitzgerald, and Duke Ellington. With his trademark trumpet at its forty-five-degree angle (which was developed when someone accidentally fell on it), Dizzy continued playing jazz throughout his life, setting high standards in trumpet playing.

DR. KWAME NKRUMAH (b. September 21, 1909; d. April 27, 1972) Prime Minister. President of Ghana. He lived and studied in the United States and in the United Kingdom from 1935 to 1945, earning a bachelor's degree and master's degrees in science and philosophy. Throughout his political career Nkrumah sought the independence of the Gold Coast (an African nation that is now known as Ghana) from British rule, forming the nationalist Convention People's Party (CPP) in 1948. He was Ghana's prime minister from 1957 to 1960, and president from 1960 to 1966. Then he was overthrown by Ghana's armed forces and required to live in exile in Guinea. He died in 1972 continuing to believe in an independent Africa.

EDWARD KENNEDY "DUKE" ELLINGTON (b. April 29, 1899; d. May 24, 1974). Composer. Bandleader. Pianist. Regarded as the greatest composer in jazz history, "Duke" Ellington (called "Duke" because of the manner in which dressed and conducted himself) composed approximately two thousand songs, covering a huge array of genres including ballet, nightclub, motion pictures, live theater, and concert halls. In 1930 he formed the Duke Ellington orchestra, which became prominent through radio broadcasts and film performances. During the 1940s he toured with his band both in the United States and in Europe. Among his most well-known songs are: "It Don't Mean a Thing (If It Ain't Got That Swing)" (1932), which came alive during the swing era, and "Take the 'A' Train" (1941). Throughout his career, Ellington won eleven Grammys, was honored with nineteen doctorate degrees, and was given the Presidential Medal of Freedom in 1969 and the French Legion of Honor in 1973. He was truly the duke of jazz.

VIRGIL "HONEY BEAR" AKINS (b. March 10, 1928; d. Unknown) Boxer. Virgil Akins was born in St. Louis, Missouri. He was a welterweight champion from 1948 to 1962, winning the welterweight title on June 5, 1958. (Welterweight is a weight division in boxing not exceeding 147 pounds.) In his career he fought in a total of ninety-two matches, winning fifty-nine.

THE CLOVERS Vocal Group. Much like the Orioles, the Clovers were one of the earliest African-American vocal groups. During the 1940s and 1950s many of their songs became top-ten hits. One of their most well known is "Love Potion No. 9" (1959). Among the group's members were: John (Buddy) Bailey, Matthew McQuater, Harold (Hal) Lucas Jr., and Harold Winley; with guitar accompaniment by Bill Harris.

Mood Indigo

it hasnt always been this way
ellington was not a street
robeson no mere memory
du bois walked up my father's stairs
hummed some tune over me
sleeping in the company of men
who changed the world

it wasnt always like this
why ray barretto used to be a side-man
& dizzy's hair was not always grey
i remember   i was there
i listened in the company of men
politics as necessary as collards
music even in our dreams

our house was filled with all kinda folks
our windows were not cement or steel
our doors opened like our daddy's arms
held us safe & loved
children growing in the company of men
old southern men & young slick ones
sonny til was not a boy
the clovers no rag-tag orphans
our crooners/ we belonged to a whole world
nkrumah was no foreigner
virgil akins was not the only fighter

it hasnt always been this way
ellington was not a street